SHY

Deborah Freedman

VIKING

Shy was happiest between
the pages of a book.

He liked to read about *once upon a time . . .*
and *in a land far away . . . by the edge of the sea . . .*
and stories like that.

Shy's favorite books were about birds.

Once upon a time,
in a land far away,
by the edge of the sea,
there was a bird.

Birds the color of jewels…
Birds who flew faster than wind…
Birds who could chirp a thousand melodies…

But Shy had never actually heard a bird.
None of his books could sing.

Then one day, a REAL bird trilled by.

She was singing a real song! It was beautiful . . .
Shy was enchanted. He longed to meet her.

treep treep troo-lee!

But Shy didn't know how to talk to a bird. What if he stuttered? What if he blushed? What if—

Then, just like that, the bird was gone.

troo-lee-lee-lee . . .

Shy wanted to follow, but he'd never been
to *a land far away*. Still, he hated to lose her!
So for the first time—ever—

Shy left home.

He made his way over acres and acres . . .
Shy felt like he was walking through one of his books,

though it was all far more wondrous
than it ever looked in pictures.

Along his way, Shy saw remarkable creatures.
And he suddenly heard—could it be?—
a whole chorus of BIRDS!

Was one of them *his* bird?
Shy listened very closely:

coo coo . . . *two-whit!* chicka-dee-dee-dee . . .

treep treep troo-lee!

It was the bird!

She sparkled! Just like the sun ... and the sea ...
Shy had never imagined the world was so grand.

Perhaps, one day, he would try to see more.
With the bird, Shy thought, he could go *anywhere*!

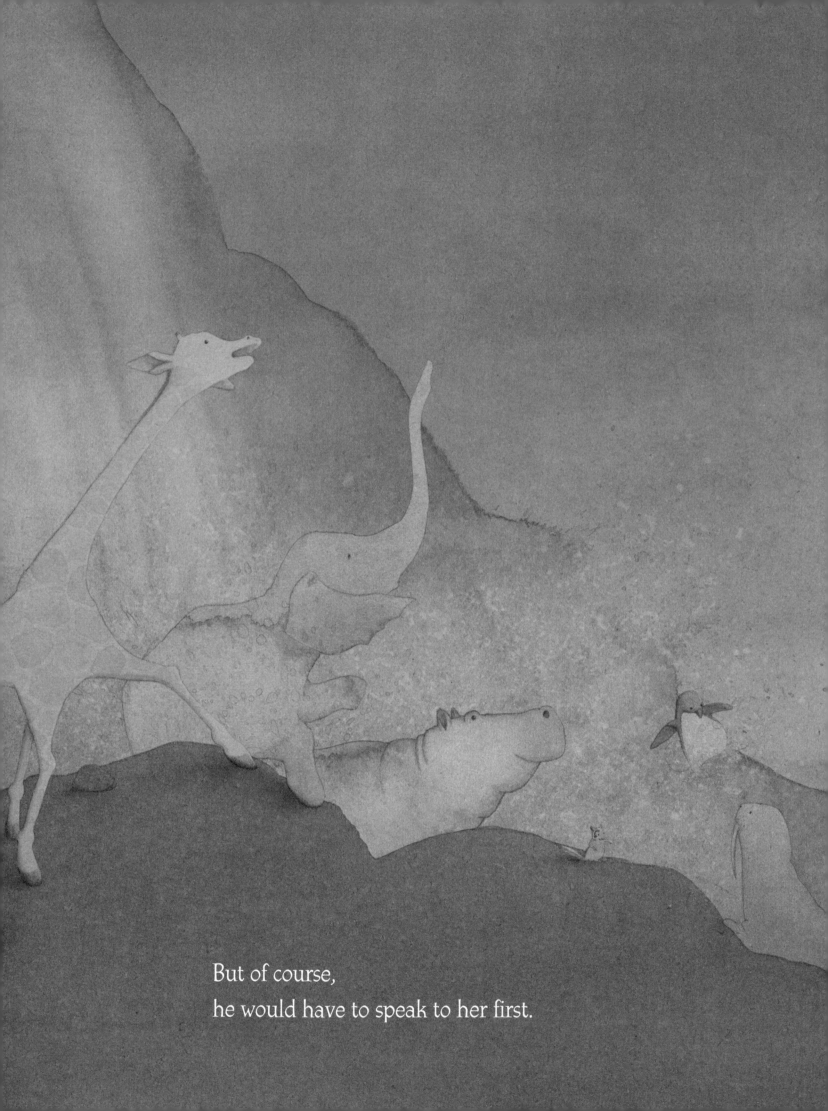

But of course,
he would have to speak to her first.

Shy took a deep breath.
His heart thumped. He looked up . . .

But he could no longer find her.
The bird was gone.

Brokenhearted, Shy went home.

He stayed awake until morning,
looking at his books.

Once upon a time,
in a land far away,
by the edge of the sea,
there was a bird.

He had been to *a land far away.*
He had seen REAL birds.

Birds colored like jewels …
        birds faster than wind …

        Shy imagined his books could almost sing …

                                treep treep troo-lee …

Treep! Treep! Treep!

The singing was real!

But it flew right by and drifted away . . .

Troo-lee-lee-lee . . . troo-lee-lee . . . troo-leee . . .

NO! Shy could not bear
to lose her again!

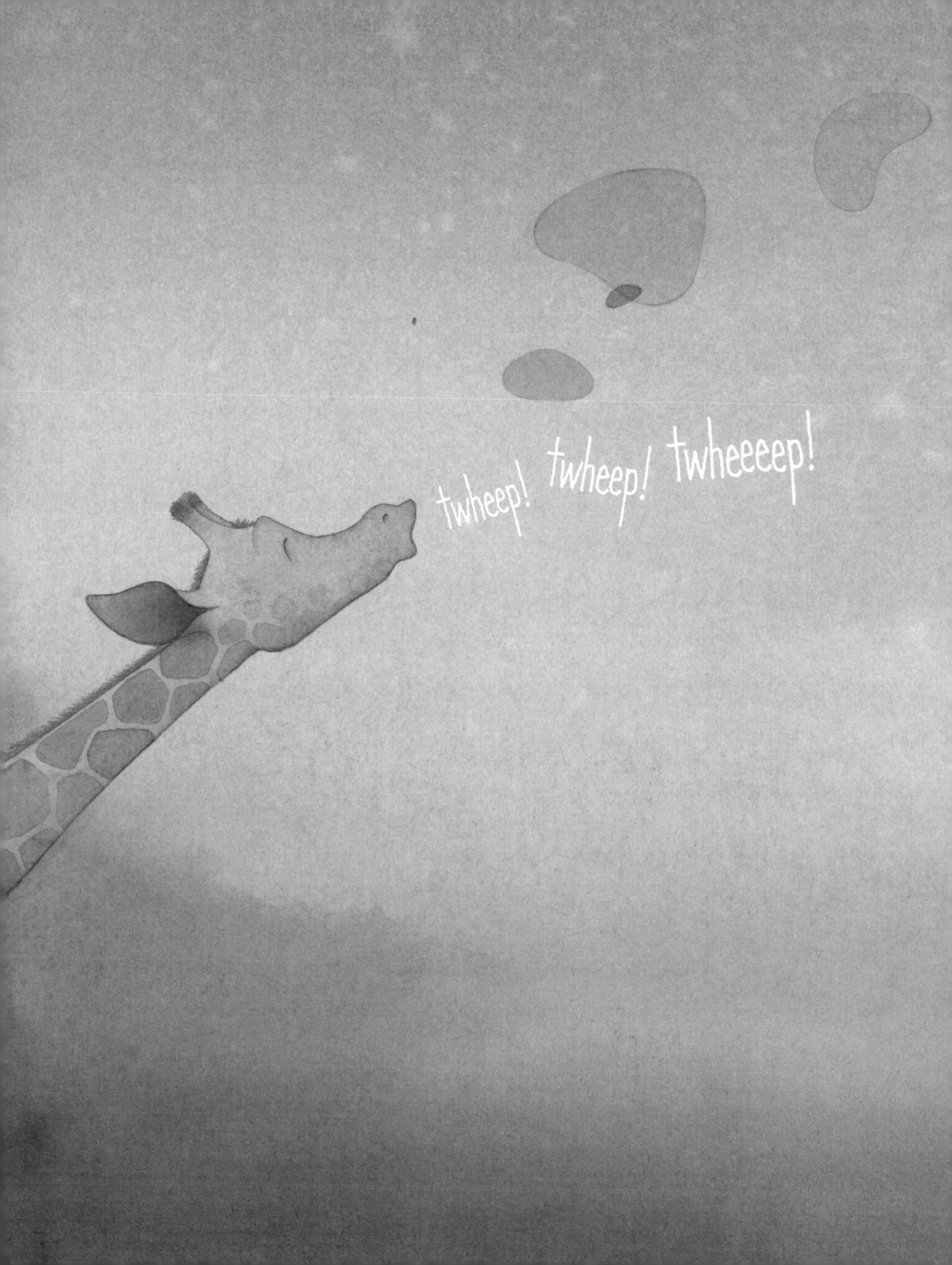
twheep! twheep! twheeeep!

And just like that,
the bird was back!

And—just like that—
Shy whispered,

I'm shy.

The bird blushed. *I'm Florence!*

And then she fluttered to Shy's book.
So Shy read to her:

> Once upon a time,
> in a land far away,
> by the edge of the sea,
> there was a bird.

More! said Florence.

Shy smiled.
There was a bird
named Florence
who found a friend called Shy.

twheep! twheep! troo lee-lee-lee...

In memory of my grandparents—
Dorothy and Milton, Sam and Florence

Many thanks to Stephen Barr, Jim Hoover, and Ken Wright—
and extra gratitude to Kendra Levin, for helping me find my voice.

VIKING
An imprint of Penguin Random House LLC
375 Hudson Street
New York, New York 10014

First published in the United States of America by Viking,
an imprint of Penguin Random House LLC, 2016

LIBRARY OF CONGRESS CATALOGING-IN-PUBLICATION DATA
Names: Freedman, Deborah (Deborah Jane), date– author, illustrator.
Title: Shy / by Deborah Freedman.
Description: New York : Viking, [2016] | Summary: "Shy loves birds, but he's only ever read about them in books.
When a real bird finally comes along, he's dying to meet her, but he's too afraid to get leave the gutter of the
book. Can he put aside his fears, step out onto the page, and get to know her?"— Provided by publisher.
Identifiers: LCCN 2015038858 | ISBN 9780451474964 (hardback)
Subjects: | CYAC: Fear—Fiction. | Birds—Fiction. | Friendship—Fiction. |
Books and reading—Fiction. | BISAC: JUVENILE FICTION / Social Issues /
Friendship. | JUVENILE FICTION / Animals / General. | JUVENILE FICTION /
Social Issues / New Experience.
Classification: LCC PZ7.F87276 Sh 2016 | DDC [E]—dc23 LC record available at https://lccn.loc.gov/2015038858

Manufactured in China   Book design by Jim Hoover   This book is set in Athenaeum Std
The illustrations were made with pencil, watercolor, and bits of colored pencil, and assembled in Photoshop.

10   9   8   7   6   5   4   3   2   1